SONGS OF Iraq

A YEAR LONG DEPLOYMENT

PAUL SHANNON

Copyright © 2010 Paul Shannon
All rights reserved.
ISBN: 144958344X
ISBN-13: 9781449583446

TABLE OF CONTENTS

FIRST PATROL	1
CAREFLIGHT	5
ROADSIDE BOMB	9
DUCK AND COVER	13
BOXCAR ONE	15
PORTA-JOHN	17
SEAL DIPLOMACY	19
MOLLY'S SONG	21
ROUTE IRISH	27
HELTER SKELTER	31
DOG TAGS	37
RED HEAD	41
AMBUSH ANDI	43
ENCOUNTER IN IRAQ	49
INCOMING	51
CUP OF JOE	53
FREEDOM BIRD	57

ACKNOWLEDGEMENT

To those who made it back, those who didn't, and those who are back but still a little lost.

FIRST PATROL

When the fresh-cut hump lands in Iraq's gritty haze,
It's the smell that stays with him, til the end of his days,
Dead animals-rotten, smoke, fresh human shit,
Savory rice cooking, truck fumes, sandy grit.

It gets in your teeth and it dries out your nose,
It reddens your eyes when the Shalma winds blow,
You can't hide from it, mingled with all the fine dust,
It hangs in your clothes, turns your bedding to mussed.

You shower off for your first night in the rack,
You sit up in your bag, the sweat pours down your crack,
Your cotton brief heavy, shirt glued to your chest,
Desert camis, boots, rifle, just to walk to the mess.

Web belt and pistol, reloads, first aid kit,
With this war's addition, the field tourniquet,
Banned by the doctors, before roadside bombs,
Why save a limb now, when it's already gone?

The twenty pound vest weighs heavy on shoulders,
Strung with compass, grenades, six mags in your holders,
Rifle in hand, and your helmet the topper,
It keeps your brain in, catches puke in a chopper.

You're told this is called, "Full Battle Rattle."
It clinks when you walk, like bells hung on cattle,
So now that you are ready, with all of your gear,
You can't help but wonder, "Why the fuck am I here?"

When the planes hit the buildings, you right away knew,
That many would sit on the sidelines: Not you,
There was something so awful about that attack,
You knew in your gut that we had to fight back.

FIRST PATROL

In high school a bully might come take your lunch,
Chicken out, always pay him, or give him a punch,
The terrorists are plotting to kill us on enmasse,
They will kill us at home if we give them a pass.

Attacks on us all, at work in our usual way,
Car payments, home mortgage, tuition to pay,
The planes full of fuel, guided missiles bought cheap,
By hijackers, passengers passive like sheep.

But how could you blame them, were you in their place,
Nothing quite so evil we ever have faced,
The murder of thousands, meticulously planned,
For maximum impact in television land.

It seemed all around us, airplanes were falling,
Confusion, death, flames, images so appalling.
Then flight 91 impacted on empty ground,
And we learned – Good God – this plane was forced down.

That those passengers fought resonated in you,
They saved thousands, and they killed the terrorist crew,
Selfless, heroic, they charged into the fray,
Know what? You do that in Iraq everyday.

Cause the fresh-cut hump, when he goes outside the wire,
Charges the cockpit, draws the terrorists' fire,
There are snipers and bombers and booby trapped cars,
Mortars and rockets launched unseen from afar.

When a bomb blows there's a distinctive, Ker-Whump,
Though half mile away, it still makes you jump,
It's not so much how the sound crackles on by,
It's just that you know: Twenty, thirty people just died.

FIRST PATROL

Wailing so ghastly as you near the kill zone,
Hear families claim corpses as one of their own,
Burned children in the crater, dead women and men,
Is this their great victory? To what is this end?

No hill here was taken, no field overrun,
You check on your buddies, they're fine everyone,
This square you are in, this once teeming market,
To the terrorist bomber, another soft target.

With the car bomb still smoking, the news crews arrive,
Get the carnage in focus, quick, carry it live,
No analysis, proportion, no getting the facts,
Push it out on the cable: "Car Bomb in Iraq!"

There's no one to shoot, though the bomber's close by,
The crowd numbers hundreds, you still feel his eyes,
He's watching for weakness, so he hides in plain sight,
Like a criminal skulking, there's no fair in this fight.

Hours later, after supper, you cough in your hand,
And it reeks like the smoke, charred flesh of a man,
You breathed it inside you, Iraq's gritty haze,
It's the smell that stays with you, til the end of your days.

CAREFLIGHT

When the choppers come in late at night,
They come low and in pairs.
And you, who're racked out in your hooch,
Should say more than one prayer.

They fly in pairs so if one goes down,
There's hope of recovery.
They fly low and dark to be over the top,
Fore a gunman draws a bead.

It takes four men to fly each of those birds,
Two pilots and two door guns.
It's bad news that calls them out at night,
"Wounded! Need a Blackhawk run."

They land in some miserable field or ditch,
Sometimes in a crowded square.
It's just amazing the places they can fit into,
They're nimble beyond compare.

In fact, they ruin you for roller coaster rides,
After Blackhawks, those are such a yawn.
For a blown up guy laying flat on his back,
Noisy angels, coming down.

Give the broken and the split lots of water,
They dehydrate very fast.
The medic hops out and slips an IV in,
Tricky in the prop wash blast.

The stretchers slide neatly into place, click,
The wounded are styled, "Pacs."
It's a bitch to be thrown around like deadwood,
Cause you got smoked in some attack.

CAREFLIGHT

In fact, the stretchers come with four wide straps,
That hold you firmly down.
It reminds you of something as the bird lifts off,
A coffin, with no lid on.

You drift in and out of consciousness,
Think about a high school football game.
See the pilot move precisely and rapidly,
Hands and feet fully engaged.

The medic crawls between the wounded on his knees,
Some guys are already gone.
It's awkward, this sudden death visiting,
Take your hat off, stand around.

When the door gun lets his rifle swivel down,
You're back on friendly ground.
It's a CASH, Combat Surgical Hospital,
Noisy angels, coming down.

The doc waits patiently on the landing pad,
He's seen this all before.
It's triage, some people go to surgical,
And some go to the morgue.

Three piles: Dead, Dying and the Wounded,
He divides you up into.
Unless you make the first and second cut,
Buddy, you are screwed!

That is when it suddenly occurs to you:
This time I might really die.
Oh God, oh my. Someone used to cradle me,
And kiss me when I'd cry.

CAREFLIGHT

When the choppers come in late at night,
They come low and in pairs.
And you, who're racked out in your hooch,
Should say more than one prayer.

ROADSIDE BOMB

We knew that we was suckered, when Sergeant Major threw his pliers down,
He got to Oh Shitting quite loudly and he savagely kicked at the ground.
Where the circuits should be was an empty box, the trigger a phone discharged,
It's a dummy went quickly around the perimeter, now our danger was enlarged.

In the ever-changing tactics of the bomber, this was what we call a *come along*,
A lure to get us out, to draw the bomb techs close, blow the real, hidden bomb.
A quick scan of the area yielded no trip wires, cell phones or a pressure switch,
All triggers for artillery shells, mines and C-4, they are this war's pungi sticks.

Of course it was dark as shit as usual, so from this moonless mission we'd go,
Mount up, off went the six Humvee convoy, we jigged and we jagged as we drove.
A click from the come along came the boom, half expected with pending dread,
Humvee three pitched up like a whale breaking sea, four of my buddies were dead.

Where have you gone, my handsome fellows?
Where have you gone, my hearty mates?
The fire burns red, orange to dull yellow,
We watch and we sit and we wait.

We knew without even dismounting, the third Humvee had hit a crunch wire,

ROADSIDE BOMB

Roll over it, scrunch, and the circuit's complete, *Ka-Boom,* then billowing fire.
Each of my buddies had a rifle, M-4, seven or more mags hung on their vests,
The rounds started cooking off immediately, then the 50's in the ammo chest.

It is the cruelest popcorn popping, and the rounds spin off to God knows where,
Reporters style this "small arms fire," scant comfort when it whizzes by your ear.
So we couldn't approach Humvee three, or put out the fire that was secondary,
We set up a quick perimeter, as in complex attacks, ambush can be tertiary.

We tried not to look inward, at what was happening to Eric, Bob, Dave and Bill,
We scanned the fields around us with night scopes, hoping for someone to kill.
The fire burned about three hours, producing a stinking and sooty black smoke,
Our eyes watered, throats burned, it wasn't just grief on which we was choked.

Where have you gone, my handsome fellows?
Where have you gone, my hearty mates?
The fire burns red, orange to dull yellow,
We watch and we sit and we wait.

We knew the air support came at dawn, Apaches with spooky front cannons,
The barrels follow the pilot's gaze, looks can kill, along with voice command.
Two flatbeds, Humvees with power front winches, to flip our buddies upright,

ROADSIDE BOMB

The melted wreck that was their vehicle, hoisted on a truck, belted down tight.

This is when we finally went to work, gathering scraps of the blown up bomb,
A circuit board here, cut wires, a length of duct tape, trace evidence to be found.
If we are lucky, we'll find a hair or fingerprint, to compare with other *unknowns,*
Then we may identify this bomber for our buddies, and his cover will be blown.

Fine men, strapping, the kind you would slap on the shoulder at the corner bar,
In an instant, they're reduced to samples that you scrape into a sterile DNA jar.
We could only hope that in the flash and clap, that sounded their final mission,
That there was a moment — *vedi, vedi, vedi, vedi* — they had their beatific vision.

Where have you gone, my handsome fellows?
Where have you gone, my hearty mates?
The fire burns red, orange to dull yellow,
We watch and we sit and we wait.

We knew they played Australian dodge ball, in which you don't dodge at all,
You stand up in the hall, one hand over your eyes, the other covers your balls.
Your partner takes whatever wind up he wants, and throws with all his might,
The object is to pop you hard, make you flinch with pain, or, maybe, fright.

ROADSIDE BOMB

If you move even a muscle, it's a do over, and he gets to throw at you again,
And so it goes until his arm gets tired, or 'til you learn to take one like a man.
It's a fine game when you are a bomb tech, because it is all about your nerve,
We're always figuring out unseen bombers, they're always throwing us curves.

We learned something this night, hard as it was on Eric, Bob, Dave and Bill,
For each tactic we develop a counter, though in doing so some of us get killed.
Unseen bombers are always watching us, thinking of ways to improve their IEDs,
They're an unnatural marriage of homicidal lust hitched to an engineering PHD.

Where have you gone, my handsome fellows?
Where have you gone, my hearty mates?
The fire burns red, orange to dull yellow,
We watch and we sit and we wait.

DUCK-AND-COVER

Why don't you…..
    Duck-and-cover,
    Call out for your mother,
    Jitterbugging on the trailer floor.

Why don't you…..
    Grab your vest,
    Throw it across your chest,
    Chinese rockets knocking on your door.

Why don't you…..
    Kick your feet around,
    Try to scrunch into the ground,
    Turn yourself into something really small.

Why don't you…..
    Hear the big booms,
    As they walk up to your room,
    "Incoming!" the early warning system calls.

Why don't you…..
    Say, "Oh, shit,"
    As the rounds so closely hit,
    These might often be a guy's last words.

Why don't you…..
    Run to the bunker,
    On the concrete you will hunker,
    Slide hard, like you are coming in from third.

Why don't you…..
    Feel the ground quake,
    As your head inside your helmet shakes,
    That's why you keep the chinstrap buckled on.

DUCK-AND-COVER

Why don't you…..
    Pull your neck in,
    Like a turtle, drop your chin,
    Stay just as close as you can to the ground.

Why don't you…..
    Hear rounds whistle by,
    As you tightly close your eyes,
    Maybe what you can't see won't hurt you.

Why don't you…..
    Wait for the "All Clear,"
    Someone's screaming over here,
    Just be relieved they did not get you, too.

Why don't you…..
    Pretend that you're fine,
    That you weren't scared out of your mind,
    Hold that pose until the warning sounds once more.

Then, again, you can…..
    Duck-and-cover,
    Call out for your mother,
    Jitterbugging on the trailer floor.

BOXCAR ONE

The Sherpa's an ungainly cur,
She limps along the miles,
Three legged, gray, like aged fur,
"Boxcar", her glides are styled.

Pointed snout on a long shoebox,
Wings on top like great big ears,
Two props that whine and ping and knock,
Takeoff's a stiff kick in the rear.

With an awkward leap, the runway's left,
The engines drag you higher,
You tap your foot and hold your breath,
"Christ, no way this thing's a flier."

The wings don't even seem to work,
Until the climbing levels off,
The turns are unexpected jerks,
The tail's armor is stiff cloth.

The seats are Baptist wake-up pews,
There is no way that you can brace,
The windows give a portal view,
Landing is like falling on your face.

And yet this homely aged mutt,
Is the Special Force's darling,
It lands on a dime and saves your butt,
When the bad guys come a calling.

Good things come in this plywood box,
Half a platoon leaps out the rear,
They're battle ready, loaded, locked,
And the props are still in gear.

BOXCAR ONE

Just 500 feet, and it's one more pass,
The pilot doesn't want to linger,
His hand is pressed against the window glass,
Look, he salutes you with one finger.

The Sherpa's more than twice your age,
So think, before you gripe her,
She was hauling guys from harm's way,
When you were still in diapers.

PORTA-JOHN

The Shitsucker man is a popular man,
And everyone knows his routine,
He drives through camp, stops at each can,
Hops out with the gear that he brings.

With his magic wand and sucker,
He mops up all that stinky crap,
It makes a soldier's fanny pucker,
As his truck completes its lap.

I've known of guys who held it in,
A full day longer than they oughter,
Just for the chance to be first in,
And splash in the clean blue water.

The Shitsucker man is a popular man,
You learn to spot him from a far,
You also must know who not to stand
Behind in line at the salad bar.

SEAL DIPLOMACY

There is a triumphal arch where the bad guys wait,
And is known throughout Baghdad as Assassin's Gate,
It straddles the zones called the Green and the Red,
People who pass through it sometimes end up dead.

There is natural high ground on three sides,
Honeycombed with alcoves where the snipers hide,
Rounds zip by you, they buzz like angry bees,
Before you hear a bang, or can drop and take a knee.

There is a twisting chute of t-walls, an M-1 tank,
Personal security details, moving persons of rank,
Long lines of Iraqis, searched on their way to jobs,
Convoys of Humvees, reporting in from FOBs.

The snipers set up after midnight, when it's inky dark,
As the morning light rises, they pick out their marks,
It is usually Iraqi, as the soldiers are behind the walls,
From a day labor line, is the one who takes the fall.

The large caliber rounds make just an awful mess,
Eyeballs roll out, big holes in gaping chests,
Try as you like, you just can't fix them up,
Their dying was fast, but, man, did it suck.

Then one day we decided that we had quite enough,
It was time to call the varsity, time to get tough,
The Seal teams arrived, sort of like a sudden wind,
Can't see where they are, and don't know where they've been.

The teams are rather small, two or three at most,
The shooter and his spotters, might as well be ghosts,
They don't shoot yet, maintain invisibility,
They watch and they wait … a patient strategy.

SEAL DIPLOMACY

Three days pass, the bad guys' harvest moon,
People still are getting killed, but change is coming soon,
Methodically and motionless, in desert boonie suits,
The Seals find their vantages, green light, it's time to shoot.

An MP who is a longtime, good friend of mine,
Was at the gate next morning, reports the weather fine,
There were five shots in succession, fifty caliber size,
So sorry bad guy snipers, it's time for you to die.

My MP buddy told me that he once saw a swan,
Hit in flight by a bus, bang, and it was gone.
Yet on frozen wing, it described a graceful, final arc,
That's what the snipers' limbs did, when the fifty found its mark.

Assassin's Gate for weeks now, has been mostly sniper free,
Thanks to what our soldiers call, Seal Diplomacy,
A politician quoted, see it's because we don't provoke them,
You silly, sheltered ass, they stopped because we smoked them.

MOLLY S SONG

I love you more than pizza
I love you more than pie
And I will always tell you
You're the apple of my eye.

Your hair is so long and silky
Your laughter is like a singing bird
When you say, "I love you, Daddy"
It's the sweetest thing I ever heard.

Your smile is my special sunshine
I will shelter you from any storm
You can come to me in time of trouble
You are the finest daughter ever born.

I once picked for you wildflowers
And wove them into your braided hair
You danced through a field of tall grass
A child of nature, without a care.

We ran up the tall hill together
We lay on our backs to see the clouds
Each one drifting by held a story
We took turns telling them, laughing out loud.

One looked like a dancing cow
Shaking to cream the milk in her udder
Another looked like a flying monkey
Hurrying home to sup with his mother.

Then came a hard-traveling elephant
We knew that because he packed his trunk
He was followed by a somber hyena
Who wasn't laughing, but was in a blue funk.

MOLLY'S SONG

Look, there is the dish, right there
The very one that ran away with the spoon
And how come, little girl, that a horse, not a cow
Is the one trying to jump over the moon?

We then played a game that's called, "Looking"
I asked, "How many shades of green in that tree?"
You watched as the light played on the leaves
And you counted, first one, than two, and than three.

We spotted two browns on the tree trunk
Gray, white, and tan on a squirrel's head
Then came what had to be a gift from God
A cardinal, singing lustily, a brilliant flash of red.

Yellow, white were the wildflowers
In shades that numbered at least five
So many blues in the sky all around us
They swirled together, like a color alive.

The next part of the game is called, "Listening"
Your eyes must be closed, no fair to peek
Listen to all the sounds that surround you
Imagine their source, that is what you seek.

Take the shades of color you have gathered
Put them to the sounds that you hear
Draw any picture that comes to your mind
The source of the sound, be it murky or clear.

Keep your eyes closed, don't you look
Tell your story now to me out loud
Match the sound with all those colors
Build creatures, like we found in the clouds.

MOLLY'S SONG

Do you hear the cricket chirping?
No, don't worry, neither do I
It's a green grasshopper with a violin
And a blue beetle with viola, passing by.

They are having quite a party
In fact, they are a rowdy, boisterous bunch
The other insects join them in dancing
You can hear them pour the mugs of purple punch.

Is that the wind shaking the leaves?
I don't think so, just listen to me
I think it is the sound of one-hand clapping
By tiny woodsmen with brown towns in the trees

They are clapping to show they are happy
Safe and sound, all, at the end of the day
Acorn soup in green leaf bowls for supper
Clapping cools it, and blows bad things away.

That croaking from down by the pond
That's the song of no ordinary frog
That is clearly the star of the frog opera
The diva, the belle of the bog.

She has a turban plumed with white feathers
Two frog lovers with wide floppy hats
Long-handled mustaches, red vest and guitars
Spanish gentlemen, I think, pursuing a lady so fat.

That humming is the dragonfly orchestra
Echoing the frog song with mandolin and harp
The bubbling is from the appreciative audience
The pond's bass, and the perch, and the carp.

MOLLY'S SONG

A huge frog on a distant lily pad
Is another onlooker quite still apart
He is old and is wise and he watches past dark
He feels the forest rhythm in his ancient froggy heart.

His wizard's hat is pointed felt of blue
With white stars and a yellow crescent moon
His crystal ball rests between webbed green feet
To his unblinking eyes forest visions bloom.

He sees far off into the future
And it is a future I hope for you
As I carry you, sleepy, down the hill
That when you are as old as I am
You'll have the childlike wonder to see them still.

The marvelous is always around you
You need only take the time to look
And listen, then build a lovely story
Or a silly one, like in this Daddy's book.

Don't forget to tell it to your darling
Open her mind to such fantastic sights
Dancing cows, frog wizards, wildflowers
Go to sleep now, I'll get the lights.

Because I love you more than pizza
I love you more than pie
And I will always tell you
You are the apple of my eye.

Your hair is so long and silky
Your laughter is like a singing bird
When you say, "I love you Daddy"
It's the sweetest thing I ever heard.

MOLLY'S SONG

Your smile is my special sunshine
I will shelter you from any storm
You can come to me in time of trouble
You are the finest daughter ever born.

I once picked for you wildflowers
And wove them into your braided hair
You danced through a field of tall grass
A child of nature, without a care.

ROUTE IRISH

Route Irish is a smart little road, between the airport and the palace it goes,
Whether you make it there in one piece, goodness gracious, who's to know?
It's like running the gauntlet, you're trying to get from point B to point A,
All the time waiting for incoming rounds, can't shoot first, the rules they say.

When the first round ricochets off the Bearcat, we call that getting pinged,
It is the noise that you hear before the bangs, off the armor the bullet zings,
Then you look for a muzzle flash, and let loose with some suppressive fire,
That means that you hose down a general area, until the bad guys all retire.

Bad guys are swarming around out there, they've ordinary people as cover,
So when you pass by a crowded square, how're you to tell one from another?
The taxi coming up on you, could be a bomber or a driver looking for a fare,
That man on a roof, is he shaking out a rug or signaling ambushers to appear?

The ambushes aren't as bad as the roadside bombs, those are pretty scary,
In a flash, a fire team becomes a pile of goo, divide in equal parts, then bury.
The bad guys are good at hiding them, fake rocks, hollow bricks, dead dogs,

ROUTE IRISH

When the road is suddenly deserted, that's a clue, the ambush's prologue.

It's a tickle when we pick up the 23 – year - olds, the State Department's finest,
They flew business class through Kuwait, had dinner, chose from the wine list.
They've Ivy League degrees, nice dress shoes, believe they can save the world,
But when they put body armor and helmets on, they're sorry looking squirrels.

We herd them into the Bearcat, brief them: Please, do not get in our way,
It is hotter than hell inside the armor plates, dark sweat stains, we all display.
The light is dim as well, only what filters through the hole filled by top gun,
Don't be offended if he steps on you, quick footwork when the ambush comes.

Then ready set go, the Bearcat fires up, the back hatch closes with a kachink,
Our passengers already look carsick, they glance around nervously, and blink,
We thread through a chute of concrete t-walls, bounce on ruts from M-1 tanks,
Then all at once we're in the Red Zone, we'll push through or we'll get spanked.

The Bearcats we're in number one, two, three, that's the airport convoy's SOP,
Spread out 100 yards for roadside bombs, weave like a drunk on New Year's Eve.
Most cars know to stay far away from us, but there a few that come too near,

ROUTE IRISH

Wave them off, put a round in the radiator, hope that inspires the necessary fear.

Because if that car keeps on a-coming, green light, it's ok for you to shoot,
If you kill a taxi driver by mistake, no sweat, the Ambo says that point is moot.
You climb the deadly force ladder, showed a warning sign on the truck's back,
Danger, Stay Back, that most Iraqis can't even read, is an awkward little fact.

In truth, if you hose down a near by car, you do not bother stopping to render aid,
Write a report that you feared for your life, attest that your shots were well aimed.
Keep your weapon pointed out the rifle port, look through narrow, thick plexiglass,
Remember our mission is purely defensive, that means they attack and we haul ass.

We don't like to say retreat or run away, we'd rather style it *Getting Off the X*,
That sounds considerably less panicky, helps us keep our sense of self respect.
We go like hell until past the point where they can hit with straight line guns,
As it happens, just when you think you're in the clear, the ambush it is sprung.

There's machine gun fire from two fixed points, a moving rifle team of four,
There comes the wicked whoosh of an RPG, good job that their aim was poor.
Our driver swerves at the bad guys as we let go, this was a good judgment call,

ROUTE IRISH

This is a complex attack, so our logical escape is consumed by a bomb's fireball.

All this crap – debris, rocks, plants, clouds of dust – comes falling down on us,
Sounds like rain on a tin roof, keep your hands in, these drops you shouldn't touch.
Then just as quickly we're out of it. We've made the Green Zone whole once more,
You can see shock on the faces of our passengers: "Holy Shit, this is really war."

The bad guys just kind of melt back into the dust, we drop off our human cargo,
All they have to do is wait to try again, they know that we'll be back tomorrow.
So if you ever find yourself running Route Irish, for heaven's sake, don't dally,
You're liable to find out the hard way, why our soldiers call it, *Ambush Alley.*

HELTER SKELTER

When we first met the training lady, she had a comely face,
That was before a killing exit wound blew it out of place.
She was dumped naked in a garbage heap, beside a local mosque,
Sexual mutilation and religion, how simply *arabesque*.

She had traveled very widely, spoke English perfectly,
She also spoke Farsi and Arabic, and she had earned a PHD.
She could have stayed in America, where asylum she could seek,
But she chose to return to her home, Iraq, help build democracy.

Her job was with the government, arranging training for new cops,
It was funded by America, but here her connection with us stops.
She lived out in the Red Zone, spent Friday steeped in her prayers,
She wore the darkened head veil, and in Allah placed all her cares.

But helter skelter come the insurgents, with trademark AK 47s,
They're going to rape and kill and devastate, claim to get to heaven.
How the young men got her scent, we can't know, without some doubts,
But to use the language of New York cops, someone "dimed" her out.

Someone fingered her as a stooge of America, a collaborator indeed,
Someone said she worked in the Green Zone, maybe at the US Embassy.
This we know for certain, when the young men saw her they licked their lips,
This is just what they were looking for, an excuse to rape some bitch.

So early in a morning, three young men with rifles burst into her house,
Claimed they were militia, hiding from soldiers: Can you help us out?
Just as it got light outside, they pushed the training lady into her car,
Claimed she was just cover, they would let her go, and not take her far.

HELTER SKELTER

Going quietly was her first mistake, and her brothers' who stood idly by,
Any cop knows: When a woman is taken by force, she will surely die.
But helter skelter came the insurgents, with trademark AK 47s,
They're going to rape and kill and devastate, claim to get to heaven.

This was a gang rape, it was a gang rape, a gang rape and nothing more,
They lined up in the hallway, so called insurgents, standing by the door.
Don't talk to me about insurgency, religion or what you are fighting for,
This was gang rape, it was a gang rape, a gang rape and nothing more.

The sexual attacks were first, a prelude to anything like questioning,
But to preserve the farce of why they took her: Sing, little birdie, sing.
For eight long days, the training lady suffered, naked on a concrete floor,
They used her until, as rapists say, she just couldn't be used no more.

What must have been really hard for her, because she wanted to live,
There was no way for her to save herself, she had no information to give.
But that didn't matter to the young men, they'd a bitch upon which to prey,
Now come the body breaking tortures, which made the eighth the final day.

They hung her by her wrists from a ceiling hook dislocating both her arms,
They didn't even bother to gag her, in Baghdad, screaming raises no alarms.
They went to work on fingers and toes, yanked out nails with a pair of pliers,

Shocked breasts and genitalia, remember, this is about perverse sexual desire.

They lingered long and brutally, over anything hers that spoke of femininity,
Burned, bruised or broke it, a confusion of outrages, undoing her delicacies.
They even hurt her with a power drill, a trick from Saddam's worst henchmen,
Drilled out her ankles and her kneecaps while holding her down, in gory regimen.

By now, there wasn't much left of her, broken bones in a blood smeared sack,
But the training lady had a comely face, so this was the focus of their last attack.
The entrance wound was tiny, back of head, powder stippling around the hole,
But the exit wound was massive, split her face wide open, made her eyeballs roll.

When they dumped her naked in the garbage heap, she had both eyeballs still,
The damndest thing was that after all, she looked surprised that she was killed.
Death unwanted and come too soon, murder victims share that look, surprise,
A devastation, and that's why the cops who care the most, end up in homicide.

A homicide dick would look at the training lady, find significance in the scene,
Get past the blood and gore, the natural revulsion, figure out what things mean.
That she was dumped in the open for all to see, is what detectives call, *Display*,

Like a cat that drops a dead bird at your feet, a boast: "Look what I did today."

That she was dumped naked in a mosque is telling, the need for her humiliation,
The last place a Muslim woman would want to be shamed, a place of veneration.
The attack on her face, its destruction, is central, and this is known as *Overkill,*
Destroy the face, destroy identity, the hatred here murder alone will not fulfill.

Take the sum of the parts of the crime scene, and it a detective can categorize,
Of what the scene tells you about the offenders, these guys were *Disorganized.*
That means that in real life they're losers, sexually inexperienced and inadequate,
Morally stunted drifters, they compensate for their failures by sexual attacks.

The only way they will ever know a woman is to drag her off and tie her up,
They can't assert themselves in a normal way, cowards, they've got no guts.
Which brings me to the drill, electric prod and rod they used to break her bones,
These guys have trouble getting it up, they're used to having sex alone.

So by looking at the crime scene, just the crime scene, this is an act we can define,
This was not an act of war or an act of terrorism, this was solvable, sexual crime.
Lots of evidence to work with here, if you take time to look closely at the scene,

While the training lady cannot talk to you, what happened to her fairly screams.

This was a gang rape, it was a gang rape, a gang rape and nothing more,
They lined up in the hallways, so-called insurgents, standing by the door.
Don't talk to me about insurgency, religion, or what you are fighting for,
This was a gang rape, it was a gang rape, a gang rape and nothing more.

DOGTAGS

Call it morbid preparation, but it's something every soldier must do,
Consider your mortality, then lace a dogtag down deep in your shoe.
It's stamped with name, religion, social, and your blood type as well,
But too late if they're looking in your shoe, you've been blown to hell.

That's okay because, as you know, the dogtag is not for you anyway,
It's for those who survive you, so they've something to honor, today.
Something to put into the ground, to put a statue or headstone over,
Something they can come and visit, when you are pushing up clover.

Dogtags are two tin plates, they hang from a chain around your neck,
They date from the Civil War, when volume of fire made corpses grotesque.
Unrecognizable, faceless, soldiers didn't want to be left such in the field,
They pinned names on backs of blouses, hoped identity this would yield.

Horse farriers following cavalry, Yankees, saw they could make a buck,
They'd take down a Federal's name, and on a washer it would be struck.
Strung on a leather thong, a Federal would carry it with him up the hill,
If he got shredded by a canister, his conceit was he'd be going home still.

DOGTAGS

In World War II, Korea, Vietnam as well, two tags hung from the chain,
Soldiers knew that, generally, this was enough to identify their remains.
One tag would be tied to your toe when dead, and one sent to your Mom,
It would come with a telegram and a parson, explain that you were gone.

That some meaty piece of you was coming home, gave some small relief,
People are tactile, they need to touch, they need a hole to plant their grief.
The tag on your toe would be matched with the one sent with your paper,
So your family would know that was you, in the bag, sent to your maker.

Battles shift, and so do tactics, and so do the ways they make you die,
In Iraq, it's gigantic, hidden bombs that blow our soldiers into the sky.
What a hump on the ground knows is the mechanics of a bomb blast,
That's why they tie a dogtag in their shoe, so their identities will last.

Did you ever wonder, watching grainy video of a missile raining down,
Why, when the smoke clears, there are all these sandals scattered around?
When the big bomb blows, what hits you first is called the *pressure wave*,
A solid wall of air displaced, so fast that only distance your life will save.

DOGTAGS

It is all about proximity, if you were too close, well, that's just bad news,
The wave hits you an inch above the ground, blows you out of your shoes.
The boot splits at the first eyelet, looks like someone cut upward with a knife,
The bottom of your foot is there inside for DNA, and the dogtag on its splice.

There are other parts of you scattered around, but most bits are pretty small,
The wave is followed by shredding shrapnel, and then last comes the fireball.
So when it comes to saying goodbye, it's the coffin lid your Mom will kiss,
You were rendered in Iraq's peculiar fog of war, what soldiers call pink mist.

REDHEAD

Her laugh is colored silver,
Her hair is colored red,
She is who I want to lay with,
When I at last am dead.

I have always loved her,
Though often from afar,
I am deep in war,
And I am called, *Khaffar*.

Non-believer, that is me,
A Christian in the East,
I am drawn to the fighting,
A lamb led to the feast.

I follow Christian values,
To wit: The Golden Rule,
Here it's a disadvantage,
Mercy, tolerance, all fools.

When dealing with a fanatic,
Remember this, so well,
You're an animal to him,
He will send you straight to hell.

Cruelty is to him a virtue,
Killing children just a lark,
Treat the women like cattle,
Hide their faces in the dark.

Find someone who's simple,
Strap on an exploding vest,
Tell him he's God's martyr,
His reward: Finally, lots of sex.

REDHEAD

Remorseless hate and violence,
Define extremist Islam,
Kill anyone who disagrees,
Recruit human guided bombs.

She sends me lovely letters,
Of her garden, shades of green,
Breathtaking in normalcy,
The quiet home that is her scene.

She calls me from the bath,
And so beats fast my heart,
There is no fear in her world,
No murderers lurking in the dark.

For this I can take credit,
I keep them pinned down overseas,
That you are safe in your home,
Thank a warrior like me.

AMBUSH ANDI

There was this pretty little blonde from Cleveland town,
Said goodbye to her mother,
She climbed aboard an airplane that was Baghdad bound,
Went one shore to the other.

To her this was to be another of life's big adventures,
She had never gone to war,
She didn't know that on this tribal land we'd ventured,
She was just an infidel whore.

Good intentions quite frankly aren't good enough,
To survive the Middle East,
If you think some neighborhoods at home are tough,
Try the *Belly of this Beast*.

Imagine opening all the cells at the LA County jail,
Hand out AK 47s,
Tell them it's not only okay to kill, rape and steal,
But will get them into heaven.

Tell them there is no emergency number victims call,
Oddly, ours is nine eleven,
Tell them it's an opportunistic criminal free-for-all,
Police hide in their stations.

It is extraordinary to see these young NGO types,
Earnest but oh so naive,
They bought off on all the build democracy hype,
Mesopotamia, finally saved.

America's very first involvement with this region,
Came from pirates, Barbary,
They claimed that they were allowed by their religion,
Kidnap, kill our sailors at sea.

AMBUSH ANDI

What awed our diplomats then was the level of atrocities,
And not just at our boys,
These people would kill, torture each other just as smartly,
Make that high-pitched hooting noise.

We sent reasonable men to their tribal land bulwarks,
We tried to talk to them,
Found out in a hurry the diplomacy here that works,
Comes at the point of guns.

Here blood feuds can rage over several thousand years,
Religious differences fester,
The leaders exhort people to keep the land and Islam pure,
The West is a molester.

The rest of the world has changed a lot since pirates, Barbary,
This just must be mentioned,
But the only thing that's really changed in the Middle East,
Is quality of the weapons.

Into this soup drops a pretty blonde from Cleveland town,
Travel name is Andi,
She called some Iraqis, told them she was meeting bound,
Come baby with your candy.

The NGOs like to use a type convoy that is called, *low pro,*
Three sedans discreetly armored,
Guns low, drive slow, don't bristle as you go, arrive so,
And trust is garnered.

A civilized technique, works if they don't know you're there,
But mull this fact over,
If you've given them time, date and route, the hard lesson here,
Concealment is not cover.

AMBUSH ANDI

Andi's meeting wasn't much, it was an introduction, really,
Meant as the first of many,
Groundwork to build institutions of Iraq's new democracy,
Sounds good, soft comes villainy.

While Andi was meeting inside, outside ambushers swarmed,
Thirty guys with guns,
Set two machine guns nests, four moving fire teams were formed,
One grenadier, ambush done.

When Andi's convoy pulled out of the political meeting place,
One turn blocked by barbed wire,
Forced three armored cars down a lane that went just one way,
Into over-lapping fields of fire.

This is a classic ambush technique, known as *funneling*,
Next step: split the convoy,
So on cue, from a nearby alley a blocking car did swing,
This ambush is deployed.

Here things get confusing, shooting, screaming, booms,
Andi's car pinned to a curb,
Her lead car, with two rifles and a driver, just keeps going,
Around the corner it swerved.

These three guys would later say they made some cover,
Began firing around the curve,
The truth is they ran away until the ambush was all over,
They simply lost their nerve.

Fire teams approached her car from two angles, triangulate,
One guy yanked on the door,
When he couldn't open it or pierce with an AK blast,
Tossed grenades under the car.

AMBUSH ANDI

The underbelly is the weakest point of an up armored car,
Shrapnel pierced the front dash,
Killed her driver and side gun outright, the seats caught fire,
Then the third car had a crash.

The trail car couldn't see the first car run, or the middle stop,
Accelerated through the smoke,
Hit her car dead on in the back, up her blonde head popped,
The trail car commander spoke:

"We must go get the principal", as he opened up his door,
Three rounds hit him high,
He sighed, collapsed back inward on the passenger floor,
Said, "Fuck, fuck", then died.

The other two fired out rifle ports, good job the armor held,
They could only fire out the side,
But they could see in front, two guys with a PK and ammo belt,
Approached on Andi's side.

They hosed down the back window deliberately from a foot away,
Until the clear armor shattered,
Fire a minute more, then for good measure tossed in a grenade,
Though by now it didn't matter.

These two guys were pinned down about another half hour,
Then the helos finally arrived,
They circled the area with their side machine guns full power,
Wave of bad guys now subsides.

When we finally got the fire out in the middle car by daybreak,
There wasn't much to measure,
A ham sized piece of meat, bone shards, watch with broken face,
Preserved her moment's terror.

AMBUSH ANDI

The bad guys have received a *fatwah* that is all their own,
It spells it out just so,
When it comes to a pretty little blonde from Cleveland town,
Darling, anything goes.

ENCOUNTER IN IRAQ

On hardest desert clay, still blooms this Midwest flower.
With smile or stolen glance, your pleasure she empowers.
Her joy in life straightforward, much as a playful child,
Truth is, when you get her alone, she's also pretty wild.

Sometimes what is very best, is what's most unexpected,
Imagine, a flower, in a war zone where you were directed.
Scent is evanescent, so you must savor this chance meeting,
Breathe her fragrance deeply, because life here is fleeting.

INCOMING

The seven thirteen a.m. incoming alarm went off again today,
The bad guys were up and circling before you were underway.
It's a little disconcerting when you are lying comfy in your rack,
And you wake up to the sound of people dying in a rocket attack.

You know by now it would be wrong to stretch and sit right up
So you roll over onto the floor, low crawl through all your stuff.
You make the wall that has the most sandbags piled high outside,
Wriggle on body armor and helmet, now you are fit to be tied.

Three to five seconds is what you've got, for decision making,
Whoosh and bang, the first round blows, your trailer it is shaking.
Because this is a moment of decision, do you stay or do you go?
Run for the bunker, risk open ground, or make love to your floor?

Rockets aren't fired singly, they run in groups of two or more,
If one hits near your trailer, another will be knocking at your door.
The first rocket is like a practice shot, its purpose is for *ranging*,
The bad guys want to be zeroed in, so this round is for *aiming*.

Once they see they're on target, the next volley comes much faster,
Rounds two, three, four, make no mistake, it's *you* they seek to plaster.
So during the one-two pause, you run like hell, it's all very dramatic,
And if you survive, *congrats,* you've just devised a military tactic.

You do your best hero leap, face-first dive, into the concrete bunker,
You find ten buddies, already there, and they are doing the hunker.
The floor is the safest place, it's six by six, sideways everyone falls,
Like a wriggling pile of puppies, dropped in a basket that's too small.

INCOMING

An incoming rocket makes a high pitch whoosh, loud and quite unique,
You freeze, close your eyes, open your mouth and you cannot speak.
The unbelievably loud *bang* that follows makes you think as you lie:
"Could this angry whoosh be the last sound that I hear before I die?"

The rounds are walking closer, whoosh bang, and five, six, seven,
Everyone is whimpering softly by the time in comes number eleven.
That one hit so near, that it's suddenly quiet, you can no longer hear,
Gunny is mouthing silently, comically, "Everyone okay in here?"

A debris cloud settles on the bunker, bits of vegetable matter float down,
All Clear is sounded, you still can't hear, but see soldiers walking around.
They look for the impacts, though this game of chance can't be influenced,
Luck and proximity make the difference between walking, dead or wounded.

You dust yourself off, slap your buddies, go back in your open trailer door,
A shaking trailer sure meant something different before you went to war,
Your mouth feels metallic, your tongue stale as from morning after beer,
That's when you realize: Well I'll be damned! You really can taste fear.

CUP OF JOE

Do you see this cup of coffee? This cup that I am holding right here?
This is MY cup of coffee, and only mine, so don't you *dare* come near.
I made it just the way I like it, one packet of sugar, one dollop of cream,
I stirred it thirty two times clockwise, and paused two beats in between.

Then I stirred it fifteen times in counter, and watched the surface swirl,
The steam rises from the cup, like chimney smoke, it twists and curls.
The aroma I breathe in deeply, two, no, three times before my first sip,
The warmth I feel on my cheeks, as I raise the cup so slowly to my lips.

Ahhh, this is a good cup of coffee, the best frigging cup of coffee ever,
And if it weren't for where I was right now, I'd want for nothing, never.
But I'm in the middle of a battlefield, whole lot of things I can't control,
But there is one thing exactly as I want, this cup of coffee I now hold.

Pretty soon we'll be going outside the wire, we'll do what sergeant says,
Hope that a roadside bomb doesn't blow, or a sniper puts us in the grave.
There are lots of ways to get killed out there, and most come as a surprise,
One moment you're joking with your buddies, then you lay down and die.

CUP OF JOE

I know a guy who is a copper, he does a lot of work with long-term cons,
Told him the trick to surviving prison life, is learning what to focus on.
Got no say in what cell you'll stay, when lights go out or when you eat,
But you can be the one, the only one, decides if salt goes on your meat.

Life in this Forward Operating Base, is like lock down in a prison ward,
You're behind concrete walls, no personal space, and often deathly bored.
You've guard towers, barb wire, bomb dogs and heavy guns to stop a car,
Institutional food, exercise room, an internet cafe and a so-so snacky bar.

The big difference, though, is apparent in what the FOB's design is about,
The bad guys are on the outside of the walls, and so all our guns point out.
Even when you are inside, you're never entirely safe tucked in your room,
Because when a fire team lobs a couple of mortars in, the warning is *Ka-boom*.

A buddy with whom I ate morning chow, he always had two boiled eggs,
He'd lay a napkin down, hold the egg 12 inches up, straddle the table leg.
Then he let's go and down it would fall, he'd cover it quickly with his palm,
He'd describe a small circle, crunch up that egg with that little roll around.

CUP OF JOE

It frankly irritated the hell out of me, but now I break and peel mine like that,
My buddy caught a car bomb some time ago, I remember him with his habit.
I've already decided that if I have kids, they'll learn to crack their eggs this way,
No matter what happens after breakfast time, they at least ruled part of the day.

So feed me whatever you want for morning chow, any kind of victuals,
But don't you interrupt me, and don't you come near my morning ritual.
Ahhh, this is a good cup of coffee, the best frigging cup of coffee ever,
And if it weren't for where I was right now, I'd want for nothing, never.

FREEDOM BIRD

The Freedom Bird uplifts you, in ways only a soldier knows,
You're getting out of theater, got all your fingers and your toes,
Three are dead, seven wounded, a couple of guys went nuts,
But you got everything you came with, you saved your sorry butt.

C-130 out of Kuwait, overnight in a crowded tent,
One more meal in a chow hall, one last time to vent,
It happens kind of suddenly, your buddies all disperse,
You're alone in a civilian airport, it's over – chapter, line and verse.

There is no squad here with you, no one to watch your back,
Checking six is just a memory, you're no longer in Iraq,
Your kit was taken when you landed, shoulder weapon too,
Another jerk in civvies, no one knows what you've been through.

You wander to the airport lounge, and knock a couple down,
You got fivers for the plane, when the drink cart comes around,
Some dude gripes: "This bloody Mary , it's not the spicy one,"
Guess this guy never suffered General Order Number One.

Hey man, things could be much worse, its best to let that slide,
A good day is when you don't have to duck-and-cover, or to hide.
The guy just looks at you, he glares, in fact, it seems you made him sore,
He must be one of those weenies that Sarge said we were fighting for.

A bad day is when a car bomb turns your buddy to a hunk of meat,
When a sniper pins you down, or a roadside bomb blows off your feet,
A bad day is when your patrol rushes to an exploded market square,
And you see all those little children burnt and broke beyond repair.

FREEDOM BIRD

It changes your perspective, you think the drinks and the flying fine,
Cause a good airplane flight is one that stays in the air the entire time.
The hotel room has a nice, clean toilet, you flush it over and over again,
And when you lay down and spread your arms, you don't touch other men.

You can drink clear water from a tap, man, that's really quite a trick,
Your not sure whether to trust it: "If it's not boiled won't I get sick?"
The hotel room's really quiet, there's no snores, coughs, burps or farts,
There're no small arms fire, booms or sudden screams to stop your heart.

You think about the guys you lost, and about the ones you killed,
They all come to see you when it's very dark, and when it's very still.
A celebration might prolong the day, so you walk to the hotel bar,
You end up alone, drunk, back in the room, playing on the air guitar.

Even in your drunken state, you look around for your rifle vest,
It's your habit to prop it on the bed, to protect your head and chest.
You can't find it, or anything else, so you curl up on the floor,
Hope your buddies will protect you, if a bomber bursts in the door.

Next morning, it's another plane, and this one seems really fast,
Before you know it, you are home, and now your war's in the past.
It happens just as suddenly, you're in a booth with your school friends,
They're happy that you're okay, but a little hazy on where you've been.

FREEDOM BIRD

You start to tell them about Iraq, but your story doesn't get very far,
Another Jody pulls up out front, and he has got a really nice new car.
Everyone piles outside for a look, and you're not sure what to do,
You were in the middle of your first ambush, seemed important to you.

When your Pappy came home from Korea, he had a few tales to tell,
He'd be halfway through at the corner bar, when a Paddy man's hand upheld,
"That's very interesting, Laddie, but I must stop you where you're at,
That reminds me o' a funny story, o' what happened to Mrs. Murphy's cat."

It has always been that most people, they live only round the block,
They have their routines and little problems, and they have to punch a clock.
All the hate and the killing and the fighting, well, that's a half a world away,
And if you try to tell them: No, it's coming here," their eyes just kind of glaze.

You and your pappy were gifted, with what's called a soldiers second sight,
It is a frozen moment that's your's forever, and it first meets you in a firefight.
For you it was the car bomber bearing down, eyes fixed in a thousand yard stare,
You peppered him and his car with rounds, he blew up, died and no one cared.

But you carry something from that in you, that you saw in the bomber's eyes,
What makes the *Jihadi* so very dangerous is that he's already dead inside.

FREEDOM BIRD

Empty vessels set loose in the world, powered by fanatical religious hate,
They kill anything they encounter, you to them are nothing, *apostate*.

That bomber is coming, he is coming, he is coming just over the hill,
You pinned him down in Iraq for a while, but you know he is coming still.
You look for him at the grocery store, in the park and at the baseball game,
You wonder if you will spot him before he detonates, kills and maims.

Your friends say that you have changed, and, you know, they got that right,
Because you know this very certainly: We can't run away from this fight.
It is no longer a matter of distance, as your plane ride home so clearly showed,
That bomber is coming, he is coming, he is coming just down the road.

Ghosts and walking dead men, that's what came home with you from war,
The former you hide yourself from, but the latter you are always looking for.
You will come to know that there is a darkness that sometimes wells up in you,
Realize that combat made you stronger, but dropped a scorpion in your shoe.

ABOUT THE AUTHOR

Paul Shannon is a 24 year veteran of the FBI with extensive investigative experience and expertise in forensic identification and counterterrorism. He has led numerous FBI missions to Iraq, Afghanistan, Pakistan and other difficult and dangerous places. He has interviewed hundreds of terrorists, and he initiated the FBI's Known/Suspected Terrorist fingerprint database. A fingerprint expert, he was chosen by the FBI to deploy to Iraq to fingerprint Saddam Hussein. He received the FBI Campaign Support Medal for extended work in a combat zone.

Shannon wrote the poems in this book while on a yearlong deployment to Iraq in 2007, during which he lived and worked with soldiers in some of the most hotly contested areas of the country. He also had deployed to Iraq in 2003 and 2004, and his experiences are pre-surge, surge and post-surge.

In 2005, Shannon was named FBI detailee to the White House, Homeland Security Council. He wrote much of the policies for the biometric screening of foreign visitors to the US and was an early advocate of the military integrating forensic work into military operations in Iraq and Afghanistan.

Shannon was a newspaper reporter with the Miami Herald, Miami, Florida, prior to joining the FBI. He also worked as a magazine writer in Washington, DC, and he was an adjunct professor of journalism at Florida Atlantic University. Shannon is a graduate of The College of William and Mary in Virginia, and he received a Masters degree from the University of Missouri in Colombia, Missouri.

THE MOON PRAYER
AKA: THE DEPLOYMENT PRAYER

By ANONYMOUS

(I learned this prayer when I was a child. I have no idea who wrote it or if I have the words exactly as they were first written. But it seems the perfect prayer to teach your loved ones when you are at longitude 44 and they are at 77. Especially when the moon is full: You can bounce the prayer off it to them, and they can bounce a prayer right back.)

I see the moon,
The moon sees me.
God loves the moon,
And God loves me.

I see the moon,
The moon sees you.
God loves the moon,
And God loves you.

I see the moon,
The moon sees you.
I love the moon,
And I love you.

Made in the USA
Columbia, SC
14 October 2023